Mimi
and the
Mountain
Dragon

MICHAEL MORPURGO ✿ HELEN STEPHENS

EGMONT

EGMONT

We bring stories to life

First published in Great Britain 2014
by Egmont UK Limited
The Yellow Building, 1 Nicholas Road, London W11 4AN
www.egmont.co.uk

Text copyright © Michael Morpurgo 2014
Illustrations copyright © Helen Stephens 2014

Michael Morpurgo and Helen Stephens have asserted their moral rights

ISBN 978 1 4052 6934 6

A CIP catalogue record for this title is available from the British Library

Stay safe online.
Egmont is not responsible for content hosted by third parties.

For Isla and Alara,
their story

M.M.

Every Christmas Eve in the little village of Dorta where I grew up, high in the mountains of Switzerland, we have a carnival, a carnival like no other. We call it "Drumming the Mountain Dragon".

Everyone gathers around the Great Bear, the statue that stands in the middle of the village square. Sounding our hunting horns, and banging our drums, and not only drums but pots and pans too, we make our way up through the streets. The children lead the way, cracking their long whips and yelling as loud as they can. Even the smallest children join in.

4

Wrapped up on their sleds, they
blow whistles, shake rattles, or
bang away on their tambourines.
We troop through the village
until we're out on the snow-covered
slopes right under the mountain,
all of us banging and clanging,
shouting our defiance, letting that
beastly Mountain Dragon know
just how we feel, telling her to
stay in her castle and leave us
in peace for another year.

*Then
the next
evening, and
of course it's
Christmas Day by
now, all of us gather in the
village square again, not with
hunting horns and drums and whips,
but with bells, sheep bells for little children,
and cow bells for everyone else. We carry flaming
torches partly to light the way, partly to keep us warm.
We go the same way we went the day before, but this
time ringing our bells. We climb up higher than we did on
Christmas Eve, right up to the tree line below the castle
walls. Here we always stop and listen to the mountains
above, echoing with the sound of our bells. Then we sing
a Christmas carol, to the Mountain Dragon, and always*

the same carol: "Sweet bells, sweet chiming Christmas bells".

Now, after the last echoes have died away, comes the time for the story, the story of Mimi and the Mountain Dragon, *the story that reminds us each year why we have our carnival on Christmas Eve, why we come back up the mountainside again on Christmas Day, and why this time we come ringing our bells and singing our carols.*

The storyteller is chosen by lottery, a name plucked from a hat. This last Christmas time it was my name that came out. I was the storyteller. Everyone hurled their flaming torches into a heap to make a bonfire, and we clustered round it.

"Don't make it too long, Michael," the Mayor told me, "or, bonfire or not, we'll freeze to death up here. Always remember the story has to warm our hearts and warm our toes at the same time."

Keeping his advice in mind, I began my telling of the story.

Mimi
and the
Mountain
Dragon

"This story happened a long, long time ago, before the first cars and tourists and skiers ever came to our little village. No one came here, except passing tradesmen, or the occasional traveller lost in a blizzard and seeking shelter

for a night. In winter-time, snow would cut the village off from the rest of the world for months on end. Families and their animals huddled together under the same roof, to keep warm, to survive. And in summer-time, every daylight hour was spent growing and harvesting corn and hay and straw, gathering berries and herbs and mushrooms from the mountainsides, fattening the pigs and sheep, making cheese, and bringing in enough firewood from the forests.

By Christmas each year they were in the depths of winter, and everyone was longing for the dark nights to shorten, for the snows to melt away in spring, for sunshine to light up the world. But Christmas for the villagers then wasn't simply to celebrate the promise of spring to come, or even the birth of a baby in Bethlehem 2,000 years before. All the singing of carols, the ringing of bells,

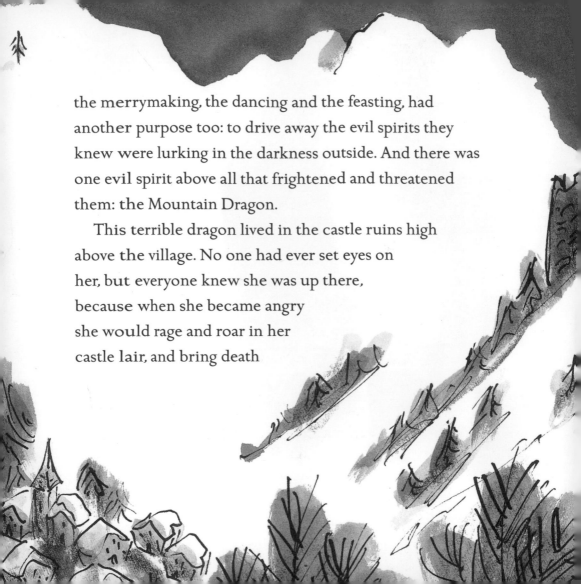

the merrymaking, the dancing and the feasting, had
another purpose too: to drive away the evil spirits they
knew were lurking in the darkness outside. And there was
one evil spirit above all that frightened and threatened
them: the Mountain Dragon.

This terrible dragon lived in the castle ruins high
above the village. No one had ever set eyes on
her, but everyone knew she was up there,
because when she became angry
she would rage and roar in her
castle lair, and bring death

and disaster down upon our village below. She would spew out fire, setting the forests ablaze in summer. And in winter she would shake the mountain with lightening and thunder, so that the snow would break loose and slide down the mountainside in huge avalanches. Many houses and many people had vanished under these avalanches, never to be seen again. And if anyone disappeared in the mountains, a child playing by a stream, a hunter out in the forest, a villager gathering berries, it was the Mountain Dragon who had carried them off to her lair in the castle.

The villagers tried everything to protect themselves from this merciless dragon. They prayed in church, they laid curses on her, they burnt effigies of her. And every year on Christmas Eve they would gather in the village square and set out for the Mountain Dragon's castle, banging their drums, blowing their hunting horns, cracking their whips. 'Do your worst!' they'd cry, when they came

as close to the castle as they dared. 'We're not frightened of you! You huff and you puff all you like! We don't care! We're staying! This is our mountain, our village, not yours!' Then they'd set up a chanting that echoed all round the mountains and down the valley. 'Death to the Mountain Dragon! Death to the Mountain Dragon!'

And this was how it went on every Christmas Eve for hundreds of years.

Then early one Christmas Day, the morning after the Drumming the Mountain Dragon carnival, something amazing happened, something so extraordinary that it changed the fortunes of the village, of all of us, for ever.

They say it all began in the year of 1314. Mimi Arquint was the only child of a farming family living in a house below the little chapel of San Bastian. That snowy Christmas morning, Mimi went out across the yard to the woodshed to fetch in the logs, as she always did. She was still only half awake as she opened the door. So it took a while after the brightness of the snow for her eyes to become accustomed to the dark of the shed.

At first she could not believe what she thought she was seeing. Rubbing her eyes and blinking hard didn't make it go away. Mimi thought it might be some kind of vision left

'I'm coming, Papi!' she called out. Mimi knew well enough what Papi would do if he discovered there was a baby dragon in the woodshed. 'Death to the Mountain Dragon! Death to the Mountain Dragon!' Hadn't the whole village, Papi along with them, chanted that together only the day before? She had to hurry. But to her astonishment, when she turned round again, the dragon was nowhere to be seen. Maybe she had been imagining him after all.

But a few moments later she heard the sound of his humming from above her head. There he was, perched high on a rafter, wings outstretched in alarm, wide-eyed and breathing hard. She could see at once how frightened he was.

'It's all right,' said Mimi. 'Come back down. I won't hurt you. I won't let anyone hurt you.' She held out her arm. 'Come on, little dragon.' Mimi knew he would come when he was ready. And so he did, floating down on outstretched wings and landing on her wrist. His claws may have been long and sharp, but he did not hurt her. As he sat there she sang softly to him, her favourite Christmas carol, 'Sweet bells, sweet chiming Christmas Bells.' And now when he hummed, it was her tune he seemed to be humming. It was his way of speaking to her, telling her he trusted her. Music was the language of dragons!

'I don't think anyone knows dragons like music,' Mimi said. 'Does your mother sing to you, like Mutti sings to me? And your mother, she's up there in her castle, isn't she, worried sick about you? And you've gone off and got yourself lost, haven't you?'

'Breakfast, Mimi!' came Mutti's voice now from across the yard. 'Hurry up, or we'll be late for church!'

'And bring that wood!' Papi was yelling.

'Coming, Papi! Coming, Mutti!' Mimi cried.

'I've got to go,' she told the little dragon, stroking his neck with the back of her finger. 'You must be starving, you poor thing. I'll fetch you some breakfast, shall I? Do dragons eat honey cake? I bet they do. I'll get you some. And afterwards, I'd better get you back home before your mother comes looking. She's the Mountain Dragon, isn't she? And she's going to be so angry if she discovers where you are. She'll think we've stolen you away or something.

She'll be furious, and if the Mountain Dragon gets angry, if she starts roaring and raging, well . . . anything could happen.'

Mimi settled him back on the woodpile, and quickly gathered up some logs. 'I'll be back soon with your breakfast,' she told the little dragon. And off she went with her logs, leaving him in the dark of the woodshed.

As usual there was honey cake and hot milk for breakfast. Mimi drank the milk but didn't eat the honey cake. She had plans for it. Mimi longed to tell Mutti all about the little dragon in the woodshed, but Papi was always there in the kitchen with them; and Papi wasn't just a farmer, he was a hunter, and a good one too. There was the bearskin on the chair to remind her, and antlers on the walls everywhere.

It was a lovely tune, a simple tune, so Mimi found herself almost at once able to hum along in perfect harmony.

As she hummed, she felt so overwhelmed with tenderness for him, so sure he would not harm her, that she reached out and touched his neck with her fingertips. At this the little dragon opened his eyes, which were as green as the rest of him, and looked up at her, not in fear, but in wonder.

'I'll look after you, I promise,' she whispered.

That was when there came a sudden loud bellowing from across the yard. It was her father.

'Where's that firewood, Mimi?' he shouted crossly. 'The oven's going out! Do I have to come and fetch it myself?'

over from some half-forgotten dream. But the moments passed and the vision was still there.

There could be no doubt about it, her eyes were not playing tricks on her. It was lying there curled up on the woodpile. A baby dragon! He was entirely green from head to tail. His eyes were closed, and he was snoring softly, a strangely soothing sound, almost as if he was humming his own lullaby. Little puffs of smoke rose into the air in time with the baby dragon's musical snoring.

'You're very quiet this morning, Mimi,' said Mutti. 'It's Christmas Day. You should be happy. And you haven't touched your honey cake. Are you all right, dear?'

'I'm fine, Mutti,' Mimi told her. 'I just don't feel like eating, that's all.'

'Wasn't it the best yesterday?' said Papi, tucking into his honey cake. 'Wasn't that the best carnival ever? We showed that nasty old dragon, didn't we, Mimi? She'll hide away in her castle all year after that. No forest fires this year, no avalanches.'

'We'll see.' Mutti didn't sound so sure. 'Every Christmas Eve we go out drumming the Mountain Dragon, but every year we still have a fire, don't we? Or an avalanche? Or someone goes up onto the mountain and doesn't come back? If you ask me, all that drumming may make us feel better, but it doesn't seem to do much good.'

At that moment the church bells began to ring. Mutti got up in a hurry and cleared away the table. Papi was putting on his coat. So neither of them noticed Mimi squirrelling away her piece of honey cake in her pocket.

Then she was out of the door before they could stop her. 'I'll meet you in church,' she cried. 'There's something I have to do first. Byee!'

'Where are you going, Mimi?' Mutti called after her. But she was gone.

As she ran across the farmyard, she could see the villagers tramping their way to church through the snow, their breath smokey on the air – just like my little dragon, Mimi thought. Close to the woodshed now, she began to hum 'Sweet bells' to let the little dragon know it was she who was coming, so he wouldn't be frightened.

She found him waiting for her on the woodpile exactly where she had left him, still snoring, smokily, still humming. Mimi crouched down and fed him the honey cake. He finished every last crumb of it, licking his lips again and again, in case there was a crumb he had missed. That was when Mimi caught sight of his teeth for the very first time, and was suddenly just a little afraid. They looked as sharp as icicles, and there were so many of them. But his eyes were smiling up at her and she knew there was nothing to be afraid of.

'I've worked it all out,' Mimi said. 'As soon as the bells stop ringing, we'll know that everyone is safely inside the church. On Christmas Day everyone goes to church, even

Papi, so no one will be about, no one will see us. Do you know what I'm going to do? I'm going to carry you home to your mother, back up to the Mountain Dragon's castle. That's where you live, isn't it?'

All the while as she was speaking, the little dragon had his head on one side, listening to every word. 'Your mother, she won't hurt me, will she? She won't blast me with her fire?'

He began humming again then, but louder, more urgently. The louder he hummed, the deeper the breaths he took, and the more he puffed out his smoke. He wafted his tail to and fro. Mimi was sure he was trying to tell her something,

And then she understood what it had to be. Everything would be fine if she hummed, if she sang. That's what made the little dragon happy, so that's what would make the Mountain Dragon happy too. Music!

The church bells stopped ringing. It was time to go, and the little dragon seemed to know it. He spread his wings, lifted off the woodpile and landed gently on Mimi's shoulder. Out they went together into the farmyard. The cows were in the snow-covered meadow. The sound of their ding-donging bells filled the air all around, as Mimi walked through the herd. Martha, always the friendliest of the cows, came wandering over to her to be stroked. But once she saw the little dragon, she stopped, looking sideways at her, and snorting.

'It's all right, Martha,' Mimi said, 'he's a dragon,

but he's only a baby dragon. He won't hurt you'. That was when the idea came to her. 'Martha, can I borrow your bell? I'll bring it back, I promise'. And Mimi reached out and unfastened the bell from around Martha's neck. She didn't seem to mind at the time, but afterwards she did follow them for a while through the snow, mooing mournfully as Mimi walked away up the mountain, the little dragon on her shoulder, ringing the cow bell and humming as she went.

'Sweet bells, sweet chiming Christmas bells', Mimi was singing out loud now, the little dragon humming along in her ear. It was a steep climb, and steeper still the closer they came to the trees and the castle beyond. She was finding it harder and harder to

keep going, and to keep singing, and it wasn't only because she was tired. Every time she glanced up at the looming grey walls of the castle, her heart filled with fear.

There was a moment when she thought she couldn't go on. She was standing in deep snow, looking back down at the village, at the church steeple, knowing that Mutti and Papi and everyone else was there.

She longed to be safe inside the church with them. She could just hear them singing 'Sweet bells, sweet chiming Christmas bells'. That sound was all she needed to lift her spirits, to give her the courage she needed to go on.

On she tramped through the snow, ringing her bell, singing out as loud as she could, the little dragon still humming in her ear. Onwards and upwards, onwards and upwards, until she found herself at last right under the castle walls, with only the drawbridge between her and the great wooden doors of the castle.

'What do I do now, little dragon?'

Mimi whispered. 'Is this where you live? Is this where the Mountain Dragon really lives?'

At that very moment, she saw the castle doors yawning open, and there at the far end of the drawbridge stood the Mountain Dragon herself, more monstrous, more terrifying than Mimi had ever imagined she could be. She stood as high as the church steeple, green and scaly from head to tail, just like the little dragon, but her brow was heavy with anger and her eyes blazed with fury. Fiery smoke billowed from her nostrils, and she pawed the ground with her great claws like a bull ready to charge.

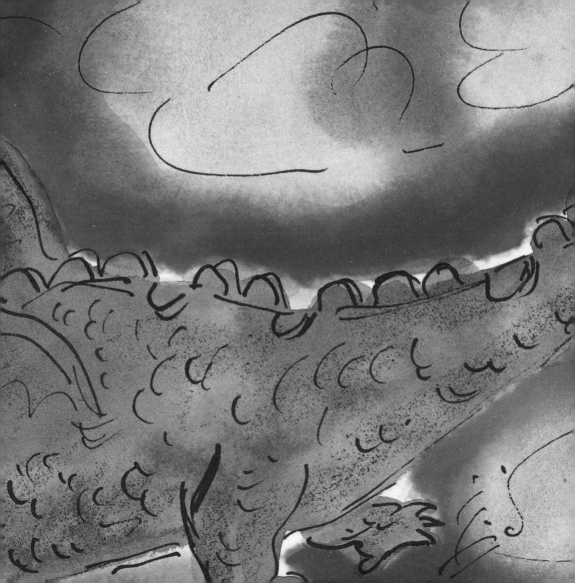

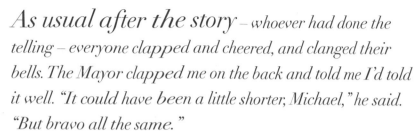

As usual after the story – whoever had done the telling – everyone clapped and cheered, and clanged their bells. The Mayor clapped me on the back and told me I'd told it well. "It could have been a little shorter, Michael," he said. "But bravo all the same."

With the bonfire of torches almost burnt out by now, we all wanted to get back to the warmth of our homes. I stayed behind for just a while longer, as I often had done as a little boy, hoping that just *this* once, I might catch a glimpse of the Mountain Dragon high on the ramparts, and maybe the little dragon too. They didn't show themselves. They never have done.

But they are up there, I know they are.

All Mimi wanted to do was to turn and run, but her legs would not move. She was rooted to the spot with terror. Any moment now, she could be torn to pieces by those terrible claws, or burnt to cinders by a single blast of the Mountain Dragon's fiery breath.

But suddenly, the little dragon began to cheep and flap his wings excitedly, and with a screech of joy, he took off. He wasn't that clever at flying yet, so he didn't quite manage to make it all the way across the drawbridge. He landed clumsily, tumbling over and over, and then stumbling on through the snow till he ended up at his mother's feet.

The Mountain Dragon looked down lovingly at him, then bent to gather him up. Gently she held him, sweetly she hummed to him. And Mimi could hear him humming back.

But now, the reunion over, the Mountain Dragon turned her attention to Mimi once more, and began walking slowly across the drawbridge towards her. Closer came those claws, closer came that scaly monstrous head, that fiery breath, so close now that Mimi could feel the

heat of it. She did **not** back away, though. She felt no need to, because there **was** no anger in the Mountain Dragon's eyes any more, only **kindness** and tenderness.

Slowly the Mountain Dragon lowered her head, near enough now for **Mimi** to reach out her hand to touch her nose. And this she **did,** because she knew that she had nothing to fear, that **this** terrifying creature could be kind and tender, like any **mother**, like Mutti.

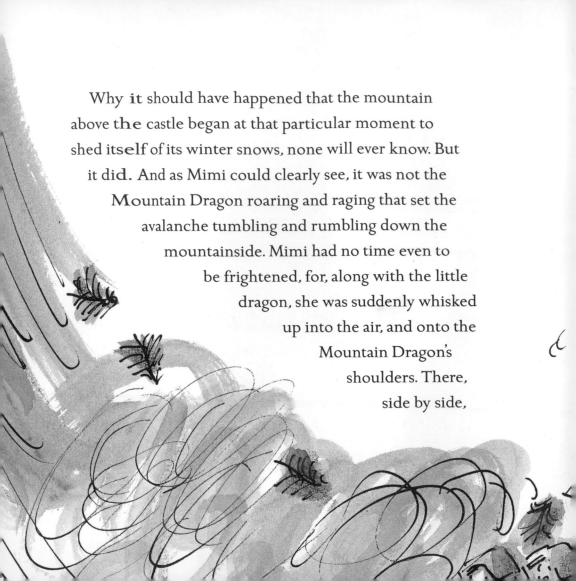

Why it should have happened that the mountain
above the castle began at that particular moment to
shed itself of its winter snows, none will ever know. But
it did. And as Mimi could clearly see, it was not the
Mountain Dragon roaring and raging that set the
avalanche tumbling and rumbling down the
mountainside. Mimi had no time even to
be frightened, for, along with the little
dragon, she was suddenly whisked
up into the air, and onto the
Mountain Dragon's
shoulders. There,
side by side,

they both clung on for dear life, as the Mountain Dragon spread her wings, and lifting off, flew up and away, high above the castle, high above the mountain peaks. Mimi could only look down in horror as the avalanche gathered speed, thundering down towards the village, towards the church, tearing rocks and trees out of the ground as it went, covering houses and barns, filling the streets and the village square, snapping the church steeple in two like a matchstick, and smothering entirely the church beneath.

All was still now, all was silent. The avalanche was over. The village and everyone who lived there were buried underneath the snow.

Mimi was yelling in the Mountain Dragon's ear now: 'Mutti's in the church, Papi too! Everyone is in there!'

The Mountain Dragon flew down, circling the village once, and landing beside the broken church steeple. She drew herself up to her full height, took a deep breath, and blasted out her fire. At once the snow began to melt away. Again and again she did it, until the roof and the walls of the church could be seen, and the windows, and

the doorway, until the first of the villagers emerged from inside, utterly bewildered and astonished. Imagine Mimi's great joy and relief when she saw Mutti and Papi coming out too.

And what did they see? The Mountain Dragon walking through the village, breathing out her fire, melting the snow all around her; and Mimi and the little dragon were riding on her shoulders. Within an hour or so, every

house and every barn was clear of snow, and the streets
ran like rushing torrents. Not a single soul died that
day in Dorta, not a horse, not a cow
(not Martha!), not a sheep, not a pig,
not even a hen.

It's true that some of the houses were
left a little scorched here and there.
We can still see the Mountain Dragon's
scorch marks on the statue of the Great
Bear, can't we? And many of the houses,
and the church itself of course had to be
repaired. But our village, our Dorta, was
saved, and all the people too.

That night, with the Mountain Dragon
and the little dragon back home in

their castle, everyone gathered in the square, not banging drums or blowing hunting horns this time, but with hundreds of ding-donging cow bells. Ringing bells and carrying flaming torches, they made their way up to the castle. And here, right where we're standing tonight, under the castle walls, they sang Mimi's favourite carol, 'Sweet bells, sweet chiming Christmas bells'.

And from that day to this, with the Mountain Dragon, and the little dragon, looking out for us and protecting us, we have never once had an avalanche anywhere near the village, nor a forest fire, and no one ever since has disappeared in the mountains.

But what does it mean, this little story of ours that we know so well? I think it means many things: that dragons need not be the dragons we believe them to be; that little

children, like Mimi, sometimes know better than
grown-up children; and that sweet bells,
sweet chiming bells can bring us all
new hope and joy and peace
at Christmas time."